Andy P

and his ho

Story by Maria Bird
Illustrated by Matvyn Wright

HODDER AND STOUGHTON
LONDON SYDNEY AUCKLAND TORONTO

IN Andy Pandy's toy cupboard there is a beautiful Hobby-horse. It has a white silky mane and big brown eyes. There are two handles to hold, and at the back are two little red wheels.

WHEN it is a fine day, Andy Pandy rides him round and round the garden. One day Andy Pandy asked his little Teddy Bear to get up behind him and go for a very long ride.

TEDDY jumped up as quickly as he could, but as soon as he was on, he jumped off again, because he said the seat was too hard.

"I MUST go into the house and fetch a cushion," said Teddy, and he came back with a very pretty cushion which was blue with white spots.

ANDY PANDY held
the cushion while Teddy climbed
on again. "Are you comfortable
now?" Andy asked. "If so, we
can start." "Wait a minute," said
Teddy, "we can't go without
Looby Loo." Looby Loo is Andy
Pandy's little rag doll.

"OH yes, we must take her," said Andy Pandy, "and we will take our tea with us as well." And they both went into the house again to fetch Looby Loo and a picnic basket.

"NOW, are we ready?" said Andy Pandy. "Are you both comfortable?" Teddy said: "Not very, because Looby Loo is so heavy." But Andy only laughed and said: "A little rag doll couldn't be heavy."

WHEN they had had a long ride, they found a shady place under some big trees. "Shall we unpack the basket?" said Andy Pandy. Right on top was a white cloth, which Andy Pandy and Teddy spread on the grass.

AND
underneath
were—
Three little mugs, and
Three little plates, and
Three little spoons.

AND a whole lot of jam-tarts, some milk in a bottle, and an apple for Hobby. Andy Pandy and Teddy laid them all out on the cloth, and then sat down to have their tea.

JUST as they were going to begin, the Hobby-horse, who was enjoying some nice sweet grass, got a tickle in his nose and sneezed ATISHOO, ATISHOO, A-A-TISHOO.

HE sneezed so loud that he made Andy Pandy and Teddy jump, and Teddy jumped right into the jam-tarts. What a sticky little bear! And when Andy Pandy had helped him to take the jam-tarts off his feet, he was sticky too.

WHILE Andy Pandy and Teddy were busy, Looby Loo helped herself to one of the jam-tarts which Teddy hadn't jumped into, and she was sticky too. They were all sticky. All except the Hobby-horse.

"WE had better wash in the pond," said Andy Pandy. When they were clean, they all sat down for the picnic. They were so hungry, Teddy even wanted to eat the jam-tarts he had stepped into.

WHEN tea was over, they packed the three little mugs, and the three little plates, and the three little spoons, and the little white cloth into the basket. And then they all rode home on the Hobby-horse.

ANDY PANDY BOOKS

Andy Pandy and the Green Puppy
Andy Pandy and the Badger
Andy Pandy and the Patchwork Cat
Andy Pandy's Little Goat
Andy Pandy and the Scarecrow
Andy Pandy's Dovecot
Andy Pandy and the Teddy Dog
Andy Pandy's Washing Day
Andy Pandy and the Hedgehog
Andy Pandy Paints His House
Andy Pandy and the White Kitten
Andy Pandy's Jack-in-the-box
Andy Pandy's New Pet
Andy Pandy in the Country
Andy Pandy's Weather House
Andy Pandy's Red Motor Car
Andy Pandy and the Willow Tree
Andy Pandy and the Gingerbread Man
Andy Pandy and the Snowman
Andy Pandy's Playhouse
Andy Pandy and the Spotted Cow
Andy Pandy and the Yellow Dog
Andy Pandy's Puppy
Andy Pandy's Baby Pigs
Andy Pandy's Tea Party
Andy Pandy's Shopping Bag
Andy Pandy and the Baby Monkey
Andy Pandy's Kite
Andy Pandy's Shop
Andy Pandy and the Ducklings

ISBN 0 340 03031 3

First published 1954
Thirteenth impression 1982

Published by Hodder and Stoughton Children's Books,
(a division of Hodder and Stoughton Ltd)
Mill Road, Dunton Green, Sevenoaks, Kent TN13 2YJ.

Printed in Great Britain by Adams Brothers & Shardlow Ltd, Leicester.

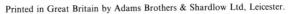